3

by

Maria Savva

Published by:

Rose and Freedom Books

P.O. Box 55285 London N22 9EU

England, U.K.

A catalogue record of this book is available from the British Library

ISBN: 978-0-9564101- 9-1

Acknowledgements

Thank you to my beta readers for taking the time to read the stories, for the great feedback, and helping me to fine-tune the stories:

Darcia Helle
Michael Radcliffe
Danille Eaves Dillon
Catherine Rose
Laura Smith
Joel Blaine Kirkpatrick
Marina Savva

Thank you to Dave Wicks http://www.opticgroove.com.au/ for letting me use your beautiful photograph for the cover.

Contents:

1

Never to be told

'I did have a sister.' Amber's eyes closed momentarily.

When she opened them and looked up at Tom, he saw the trace of a tear that appeared to be trapped in time. He gathered the topic must be an awkward one for her, and what she was about to relate held painful memories—something she found difficult to talk about even after telling it maybe a thousand times. He sensed all that from the way she sighed, opening and closing her eyes; but an apparent determination seemed to be urging her to continue, to speak this unspeakable thing. Or maybe she was debating whether or not to talk about it. The silence in that pause gave birth to so many thoughts; Tom opened his mouth to say something in an attempt to stop the deluge of chatter in his mind, but Amber began to talk again.

'She... disappeared. When she was ten,' her voice broke as she revealed this disturbing fact. 'They never found her.'

When Amber lowered her eyes, it appeared that she had finished speaking and no longer felt the desire to elaborate; but then she looked up, an urgent need to tell him written in the clenching of her jaw. The story was on the tip of her tongue, the suspense palpable; but she closed her mouth before the words escaped, unwilling to set them free. She shook her head, a hand going up to her eye instinctively to wipe away the tear that could not be shed.

Tom's throat felt dry. He regretted asking her if she had any siblings. It was something to say, a way to get to know her. First dates were always so full of uncertainties. He'd tripped right onto a mine this time. The explosion in his brain created a wave of panic. *Must change the subject, must change the subject.*

'Do you want dessert?' she asked, with a half-smile, but her brow furrowed; evidence that thoughts of her lost sister still remained uppermost in her mind.

At least she wasn't talking about her anymore. A brief sigh left his lips. Relief. But the spectre of curiosity that had been stirred in him by the way she'd answered the question remained, hovering in wait. Tom could not help but wonder. He felt an urge to ask more, but at the same time wanted to erase the initial question and her answer. But delete keys didn't exist in real life. Consequences ensued from any errors. He'd learnt that years ago.

'I'm full,' he announced, patting his stomach in response to her question. 'If it's all right with you, I'd prefer to get the bill.'

'Y...Yes, okay,' she said, her eyes reaching out to his in a gaze that told him she craved to know what she'd said to make him want to leave... Would they see each other again?

It was always the same whenever he met someone new; walking on eggshells, scared they'd discover his secret. Amber left him feeling insecure. Apprehensive. If they did see each other again, this invisible weight would hang over every subsequent meeting. He'd want to ask more, just to be sure. She'd maybe mention her sister and open the floodgates to painful recollections of his own past.

He didn't know why he put himself, or the women he dated, through it. Inevitably, something they said would trigger a negative emotion and he'd have to end the relationship. Maybe he simply didn't feel worthy; but then why did he keep trying?

'I hope I didn't put you off... talking about my sister.' She avoided his eyes, twisting the stem of her empty wine glass between her fingers. 'I should have just said I haven't got a sister. I didn't mean to make you feel uncomfortable.'

Tom's eyes widened but he hid his fear with a forced smile. 'You didn't...' He inwardly squirmed, worried that something in his demeanour had betrayed the guilt inside. Could she see it written on his face?

Paranoia, there it was, rearing its ugly head again, making it all the more important to him that he nipped this relationship in the bud.

Amber pursed her lips, then smiled at him, sadness still prevalent in her expression. With closed eyes, she said, 'I never learn.' She appeared much brighter on opening her eyes, and leaned towards him: 'Look, I promise I won't mention Molly again. It's in the past. I know it freaks people out when they hear how she disappeared; they always assume I'll have issues, but I promise you I don't talk about her all the time... She's not some ghost that will be hanging over us. It's in the past.'

Her repetition of "it's in the past" resounded in his head, along with the name, *Molly*. How could it be true? Was she the same Molly? His mind flashed back to the winter day, so far away in his memory as to be lost in the shadows of time. The mention of the name triggered the flashback. "*Molly*"...

'I dare you to walk on it!' said Tom. Life was full of dares these days; many were dangerous, but pushing things to the limit felt good. He found it funny when his parents and teachers agonised over the latest things the children got up to.

Last week, Tom had dared Jason Wright to jump off the top of the stairs; he'd done it, but smashed his forehead into the beam that ran across the hallway. He'd been rushed to hospital. Drama. The children loved it. The teachers despaired.

The week before that, Susan McGuire dared Sylvia Braithwaite to hold her breath for five minutes. Sylvia turned red and then purple, but wouldn't give up. The forfeits for the dares were even more dangerous than the dares. No one wanted to do a forfeit. Sylvia fainted and was rushed to hospital. The children found it exciting. The teachers couldn't understand the madness that had taken hold.

Tom stood there in the park with Molly Reynolds. He'd bumped into her by chance whilst out on an errand, and he'd reminded her that she was the only one in their gang who hadn't done a dare.

They walked through Gainsborough Park on the freezing winter afternoon; he on his way to the local shop to buy a loaf of bread for his mum, Molly on her way to a friend's house. He couldn't resist daring her to walk on the lake. It was frozen solid.

'No way!' came her reply, echoing in the icy stillness of the quiet park. Everyone else in the world seemed to have stayed at home today, not brave enough to venture out in the sub-zero temperatures. 'The ice might crack. It's too dangerous!'

'Scaredy cat!'

'You do it then!' Molly grinned at him.

'You're the one who hasn't done a dare.'

She looked at the frozen water, and then back at him, squinting in the brightness of the sun reflecting off the white snow, so that he couldn't be sure if the squint was a frown or whether she was still grinning. 'Okay, I'll do it... but then you have to!' She stepped out onto the icy lake slowly, steadily, testing the solidity of the surface below her feet.

Tom watched in awe as she found her footing on the shimmering ground. She twisted around like an ice-skater, and then turned towards him, a big smile on her face. 'C'mon, it's easy! Fun, actually!'

He considered it for the briefest of moments.

Then the crack, and the sound like thunder as the ice broke. Her scream erupted in the hollow air; that deafening sound in the still of silence, no one else around. His scream joined hers, and then the splash and she was gone. Tom looked this way and that trying to find an adult, someone who would know what to do. He mouthed her name but the sound didn't escape. It remained inside, afraid.

He recalled the head teacher, Mr Wilson, speaking to them in assembly after Sylvia fainted: 'Holding your breath, even for a few minutes, is dangerous. You need air to breathe, to live. It can be fatal'.

He imagined Molly holding her breath in that dark, freezing cold water. How long would she survive? One minute, two minutes...

Perhaps she was dead already.

He blamed himself. He was the one who dared her to do it.

Trauma became a living, breathing, life partner. The sense of guilt grew year by year. His conscience continued to blame him, adding chains to his back, like those carried by Marley's ghost in *A Christmas Carol.*

*

Amber and Tom were introduced at a party recently. His friend Clark said she came from the same part of London as Tom. They'd have a lot in common, he'd said. It seemed they had too much in common. Molly. But how? He'd been running from that day all his life. Should he go to the police and tell them what really happened? He'd be implicated now, surely, even though back then all he had been was a frightened ten-year-old. Molly would have no doubt died within a few minutes; it was unlikely anyone could have saved her. All he had been guilty of was keeping the truth from them. They wouldn't see it like that.

Over the years he justified it all to himself; tried to forgive himself. He'd often heard that in order to move on in life you have to forgive the child in you for what you did when you were too young to know better. By the time he did know better, he was too scared to say anything for fear of being locked up. And so it went on. An innocent child turned into a guilty adult. The years in between were cloudy with unpleasant thoughts and fears. Years of wanting to tell but not wanting to wake the sleeping dogs.

He watched Amber as she nervously twisted the empty wine glass, her eyes darting from the glass to him and then back to the glass. She seemed as lost as he was. Molly's hair had been the same light brown with natural blonde highlights. Her blue eyes were the same. How had he not noticed the resemblance before?

Distant memories, snippets came back to him, and he remembered Molly telling him about her annoying little sister, Amber. She was a few years younger; must have been about six when Molly "disappeared".

No one knew he'd met up with Molly that day. Their fateful meeting was an unexpected one, and they'd decided to walk together through the park. The lake, glimmering in the sun, looked so enchanting.

Unable to block the mental barrage of images from the past, Tom sighed as he tapped his PIN into the keypad, avoiding eye contact with the waitress who stood beside the table.

He caught Amber's eye a couple of times; she appeared to attempt smiling at him while a frown remained, as though her forehead were permanently fixed in that position. Only dejection smiled out from her face.

He knew they would not be seeing each other again. First date, last date. She didn't know why her sister never returned home twenty years ago. He would not be the one to tell her.

Agreeing to go out with her had been a mistake. As soon as he'd heard she came from the same part of town, he should have made an excuse and walked away. He'd moved out of town years ago so as to avoid seeing the same faces every day; the ones who had known him as a child but not known what he had done.

Molly never made it to her friend's house. A search party later that evening didn't find her. The girl's disappearance remained a mystery to all but Tom and the lake that kept its secrets well. He'd gone to the shop. Bought the bread. Gone back home. Carried on.

2

The Bride

Olivia drifted into a warm, contented sleep. Today, Rod had finally proposed. '*Will you marry me?*'*;* the scene replayed in her mind and she smiled to herself. She'd been waiting to hear those words for months, ever since deciding that she wanted to spend the rest of her life with Rod. She hadn't mentioned it to him, though, fearful of scaring him off. No one wanted to get married anymore, did they? These days, people mostly cohabited. But the childhood dream stayed with Olivia into adulthood; to get married wearing a fancy, white dress, and be the centre of attention for a day, like the princesses in the fairy tales she used to read as a child.

Happily ever after. There was a kind of magic she associated with weddings, almost as though she expected that the ceremony would guarantee eternal bliss for her and Rod. She sometimes thought their happiness depended on it; waited, frozen, unmoving, until they walked down the aisle as man and wife.

When she first found out Rod had been married before, it put a slight damper on her dreams. She'd assumed he had always been single. He'd married and divorced, which more or less negated her belief that marriage created happy-ever-afters; but Olivia preferred to stay positive. She loved Rod and didn't doubt that true love existed.

'We met at school, married too young, and grew apart,' he'd explained, when telling her about his first wife, Lucy.

She wasn't his true love, Olivia surmised.

Now they'd found each other—were going to get married—and the world around her held an ethereal quality.

At 3 a.m., Olivia woke up shivering. She sensed a chill in the air, as though it were the middle of winter, and pulled her cotton sheet over her shoulders wishing it were a duvet or a blanket. It was August and had been a hot day. The temperature went up to thirty-two degrees Celsius, and the weather forecast said it would be a muggy night. *Maybe I've got a fever.*

Placing a hand on her forehead, instinctively, she noticed her palm felt cold and clammy. Just then, a ball of light appeared at the end of the bed—amber then turning white; bright, but not too bright to look at without squinting. Feeling no fear, only a calmness that momentarily took away any other sensations, she sat up in bed and leaning on her elbow tried to take a closer look, but the light quickly faded.

Olivia began to wonder whether this was some kind of lucid dream, or whether she *did* have a fever which had caused a hallucination. She was about to lie down and try to go to back to sleep, dismissing the vision as imagined or the remnant of a dream, when from the corner of her eye she saw something move; a shadow in the dark. The chill that had seemingly been dispersed by the ball of light now returned. She rubbed her goose-pimpled upper arms frantically in a vain attempt to create warmth.

'Don't be scared,' a whispering voice sounded out from the darkness. 'It's only me. Jennifer.'

The voice faded into what sounded like a song... a nursery rhyme perhaps; but Olivia could not make out the words. Like a lullaby, its effect was to induce sleep. Her dreams were full of childhood flashbacks: she saw herself with Jennifer, her best friend from school; hazy recollections of the times they had spent together, the games they'd played.

When Olivia awoke in the morning, she didn't remember the ball of light or the whisper; only the dreams of Jennifer. A smiled curled on her lips. She had not seen her friend for about fifteen years—since they left primary school—but they were once so close. Olivia resolved to try to find Jennifer and invite her to the wedding. They used to play at being brides when they were children.

*

As Olivia walked along Firhurst Avenue, a myriad of memories cascaded like a kaleidoscope in her mind, and a sense of nostalgia took hold. Years had passed since she'd last been in this part of town.

She stopped in front of the gate at 55 Firhurst Avenue, a house she'd often visited as a child. Would Jennifer still live here? Maybe her parents did.

An hour later, Olivia exited the wooden door and hugged Mrs Taylor, Jennifer's mother.

'It was lovely to see you again; I just wish it had been in happier circumstances,' said the older woman. The rims of her eyes were red, as though she'd never stopped crying, not once in nearly fifteen years.

Mrs Taylor had told Olivia how Jennifer died. She'd been eleven years old. They'd taken a trip to Spain for the summer break, and Jennifer was run over by a speeding car when they were crossing a road.

'She looked in the wrong direction for cars. They drive on the right hand side over there,' said Mrs Taylor, frowning. 'It was too late for me or her father to stop her. And that car... Well, it happened so quickly.'

Photographs of the child Olivia once knew were smiling from the walls of the living room. School photos sat on the mantelpiece; images trapped in time. Candles added an eerie quality to a picture on the sideboard. The home had become a shrine of sorts.

'I remember you two playing in here for hours,' Mrs Taylor had said as they stood at the entrance to the room that was once Jennifer's bedroom.

For Olivia, walking into the room was like entering a portal to the past. Everything looked the same as she remembered. It jogged her memory so much as to become practically intolerable, given that she knew she would never see her friend again.

The Barbie doll dressed as a bride lay on the pink quilted bedspread, as if discarded after a game. The doll's arms were outstretched, her hair unkempt. Jennifer was always *Bride Barbie* when they played together. Olivia usually ended up having the Barbie who looked like she was going shopping, dressed in boots and a skirt, carrying a basket. She'd begged Jennifer endlessly, asking if she could be *Bride Barbie* just once. Jennifer finally caved in the last time they'd played together. Olivia recalled the thrill of holding that doll in her hands and walking it along the pretend aisle with the Ken doll. A tear came to her eye.

She couldn't help wondering whether fate played a role in separating her from Jennifer so that she would not have to grieve over the girl who had been the closest thing to a sister she'd ever had. Even though they drifted apart, she often thought of Jennifer over the years, always intending to contact her but just never taking that step. As the memories flooded back, she reached out towards the doll, wanting to hold it again, to feel closer to her once best friend who had been taken away so young.

At that moment, she felt Jennifer's mother's hand on her shoulder. 'Please don't touch anything, dear. I don't want to move anything.'

As Olivia twisted around to face the older woman, she could see what looked like fear in her eyes; fear of something in the room being moved and causing everything she held dear to crumble. Apparently, she had an irrational belief that keeping everything exactly the same would make a difference; as though she expected Jennifer to return. Olivia nodded and lowered her eyes. She understood.

Only then did Olivia notice the dust and cobwebs covering everything, and the floating particles of dust that could be seen as the sunlight broke through the yellowed and fraying net curtains. She sneezed a few times and Mrs Taylor took her hand, leading her out of the room.

*

Walking away from the house, Olivia tried to make sense of what she'd heard and seen. Disappointment and grief vied for attention. She felt a chill, remembering her dreams of Jennifer the night before.

Shaking the negative thoughts from her mind, she tried to focus on the positive, looking down at her ruby engagement ring, wishing Rod was there. Almost on automatic pilot, she called him on her mobile, wanting to hear his voice.

'Hello, Liv.' His tone sounded subdued.

'Hi. Are you okay?'

The brief moment of silence that followed worried her.

'There's something I haven't told you,' he said.

A multitude of thoughts whizzed around her mind—the main one was concern about the engagement. A paranoia took over: perhaps after sleeping on it he had decided that getting married again wasn't a good idea.

'Wh... What is it?'

'We should meet up. I can't tell you over the phone.'

*

Two hours later, Olivia sat next to Rod on the sofa in his flat. In front of them on the coffee table there was a photo album. Olivia noticed it as soon as she entered the room because she'd never seen it before and it stood out. It didn't fit in with the rest of his belongings. Everything in the flat, from the walls to the curtains to the furniture and personal items, was either black, brown, navy, grey, or white—minimalistic and sharp; typical of a bachelor's flat, she'd thought. This photo album with its pink border, orange and yellow flowers, and picture of a flower-fairy, looked out of place.

Tearing her eyes away from the elephant in the room, Olivia looked at Rod and noticed, for the first time since she arrived at the flat, the redness around his irises, and puffiness around his eyes; signs he'd been crying. This made her even more anxious about whatever he was going to tell her.

'Rod, what's happened?'

He sighed deeply and rubbed his hand on the armrest of the black leather sofa, eyes focussed on the photo album. 'This morning, I met up with Lucy.'

Olivia imagined he would tell her they'd decided to get back together. 'Wh... Why? I mean—'

'Wait, let me explain.' He sat forward on the sofa, leaning towards the coffee table, eyes still fixed on the photo album as though it were giving him strength.

Did Lucy give him the album as a reminder of all the good times they'd spent together? Olivia shuffled along the sofa slightly, increasing the gap between them; an involuntary reaction rather than a conscious decision. Her heart began to beat a bit faster and she looked at her ruby ring, almost willing it to protest.

'Lucy and I had a daughter.'

Olivia's eyes widened.

He picked up the photo album and flicked to the middle. 'She died in a car accident four years ago. I blamed Lucy, she blamed me. It kind of caused our break up.' He shook his head and blinked, giving the impression he was trying to banish unwanted recollections. 'Well, anyway, today we went to our daughter's grave. It's the anniversary. We always go.'

'I had no idea—'

'I know... I'm sorry. Maybe I should have told you before. It's hard to talk about.' He seemed unable to meet her eyes. 'But I thought you should know this about me, as we're getting married.' A tear rolled down his face.

Olivia leaned forward and hugged him. She felt his tears against her cheek. He was shaking.

After a few minutes, he leaned back still holding the photo album open in front of him. Slowly, his trembling finger pointed to a photograph of a happy young girl holding a doll. Golden curls...

Jennifer. Olivia's eyes blurred so she could not focus. 'It's Jennifer,' she said aloud, unable to contain her thoughts.

'H... How... do you know her name?'

Olivia shrugged, and blinked away a tear.

'That's my daughter, Jenny,' he said. 'She died when she was eleven. How did you—' His face became redder, his tone of voice accusatory.

'I don't...' She shook her head. 'Sorry... I just thought she looked like somebody I used to know.' Olivia's tears began to fall freely now and her eyes were drawn to the doll in the young girl's hands... *Bride Barbie.*

3

What The Girl Heard

'So the little girl slipped the juice from the poisonous berry into the giant's drink, and he took a huge slurp and fell down onto the floor, dead! The end.'

'Wow.' Minnie's little eyes sparkled with delight as the fairy tale came to an end. 'Can you read it again?'

'No, it's late; you have to go to sleep,' said Victoria.

'But I like it.'

'We'll read it again the next time I come, I promise, sweetie. You go to sleep, because your mum and dad will be cross if you're still awake when they get home.' She tucked the blankets into the side of the bed and kissed Minnie on her forehead.

'If someone is being angry like the giant and wants to kill you, you have to play dead,' said the little girl, quoting a line from the book.

Victoria frowned; perhaps "*The Giant and the Poison Berry*" hadn't been the best choice of bedtime story. She didn't want to give the child nightmares. Why did children's stories contain such violence? It seemed there was always at least one evil character out to kill someone.

'That's right.' Victoria humoured her: 'If you play dead, they won't hurt you anymore.'

Half an hour after Victoria put her to bed, Minnie wandered down the stairs saying she wanted a glass of water. After drinking a few sips, she said, 'Can we play hide and seek?'

'No, it's bedtime.'

'But... just one game.' The little girl looked up at her, lips in a sulk.

Victoria never could resist Minnie's requests. 'Oh, go on then, but only one, because if your parents catch you out of bed when they get home, they'll tell me off for keeping you up.'

'Yay!' Minnie danced around. 'I'm counting, you're hiding!' She ran towards the front door, stood facing it, and began to count, 'One, two, three...'

Victoria couldn't help smiling to herself. She went into the living room and hid behind the sofa.

*

Perspiration gathered on Victoria's brow, chills ran through her. She felt sure she would faint, but could not allow herself to lose consciousness; had to stay focussed. One move and he would find her. A risk she couldn't take.

He was sitting on the sofa. She could hear the old springs creaking as he moved. A sniffling sound. Was he crying? Maybe he regretted what he'd done. If he did, he wouldn't be a threat to her; she'd be able to leave tonight, he'd be too deep in regret to care. But she couldn't be sure, daren't move.

Her heels and ankles were feeling the strain as she remained crouched in her hiding place. He knew she was babysitting tonight; or could he be too drunk to remember? Fear taunted her; he might be waiting, sitting there on the sofa—maybe he thought she was upstairs. As a potential witness, he'd have to get rid of her. She'd be his next victim. Tickly sweat began to drip down her forehead in beads. She felt a great urge to wipe it away, but clenched her jaw and tried to think of other things. Even breathing was risky now, so close to this man... this murderer.

Minnie had been counting behind the front door when the door swung open throwing her a few feet towards the staircase. A loud bang, a shriek from the child, and then nothing. Victoria stood up from behind the sofa and saw Minnie lying on the floor in the hallway; she appeared peaceful, as if asleep. Victoria's hand went up to her mouth to stifle the scream that threatened to erupt. Something told her to stay silent.

She witnessed the scene as Minnie's mother Jane fell onto the floor next to the child. Then, hearing a man's voice, she instinctively knew that Evan—Minnie's dad—was responsible.

Jane Baker's screams and tears were overwhelming as she reached towards her daughter. Victoria watched on, hoping this was just a nightmare.

'Look what you've done, you bastard! Minnie! Minnie! Wake up!' Jane shook the child who remained unresponsive, like a rag doll. When she raised her tear-stained face, her eyes met Victoria's. She froze for a brief moment then waved her hand surreptitiously, indicating to Victoria that she should hide.

A sense of danger gripped Victoria and she immediately sat back down. Her mind could not quite shake the alarming image of Jane, sitting there in the hallway, mascara running down both cheeks: she resembled a haunting Pierrot clown. And Minnie... poor innocent little Minnie who had only wanted to play a game of hide and seek, caught up in all of this.

Victoria's reverie was halted when she heard another outburst from Jane; she was blaming her husband for hurting Minnie, but from what Victoria could gather, he was responding by hitting and kicking her. He began a tirade of his own, saying she was a bad mother. The verbal battle and expletives became louder. Victoria covered her ears, not wanting to hear it. She had always been a bit frightened of Evan, although she never knew why; she hadn't, until this day, imagined he could be capable of killing.

That was then. Over ten years ago.

Victoria walked along Turner Avenue holding her new boyfriend's hand. As they approached the vicinity of Number 25, she gripped his hand more firmly.

She never went back to the Bakers' house after that night.

Jane phoned her a week later asking if she could babysit again: 'Sorry about the last time. Evan was drunk. He was on meds for a chest infection and they reacted with the alcohol. He was ever so sorry the next day. He'd never hurt Minnie... never!'.

Victoria made an excuse, said she needed to study for exams. She avoided all further calls from the Bakers, preferred to keep her distance

Whenever she saw the family in the neighbourhood, she would smile politely and rush past, making some excuse or other about being busy. Her heart went out to Minnie; she wanted to get the child away from that house.

Over the next five years, the Bakers had more children. Often, Victoria would notice bruises on Jane's arms, and suspicious marks on her face that looked as if she'd tried to cover up a black eye or a split lip with make-up. Victoria also spotted bruises on the children as she walked past them sometimes, but never said anything; kept it all inside.

On seeing the children, she always felt that same pull towards them, wanting to get them away before anything bad could happen.

Victoria had moved out of town a few years ago. Now she was back because Adrian's parents lived here.

She'd met Adrian, her boyfriend, at a friend's birthday party. They'd clicked instantly.

Until this morning, she'd had no idea that his parents lived in Turner Avenue. She couldn't help but wonder whether the Bakers still lived at Number 25, and whether Adrian knew them.

'Here we are,' said Adrian, breaking into her thoughts.

He opened the gate leading to 42 Turner Avenue, almost directly opposite Number 25. Holding out an arm, he invited her to enter through the gate.

Victoria's eyes were drawn to the house across the street. Then, putting on the best smile she could muster, she turned to face Adrian and began walking with him towards his parents' front door. She took in the bright colours of the flowers on the hedge, trying to rid her mind of the darker thoughts threatening just below the surface. 'Nice garden,' she said.

'Yeah, my dad's a keen gardener; has an allotment too.'

Victoria spent a pleasant afternoon getting to know Adrian's parents. Her eyes and her mind wandered a few times out the window and over to Number 25, as if it held mystical qualities.

*

'I don't visit this area much anymore,' said Victoria, as they left the house after saying their good-byes to Adrian's parents.

'I remember I couldn't wait to leave,' replied Adrian. 'I'm always telling my parents to sell up and move to a nicer part of town—too many druggies round here—but they're old and set in their ways. Anyway, it's not as bad as it used to be. Quite a few of the problem families have moved out of the area.'

Problem families. She wondered whether that included the Bakers.

'I prefer living in Herts. Too many people in London these days,' she said.

'Yeah. It's overcrowded, that's for sure.'

They walked further away from Number 25 and the grim secrets it held. With every step, Victoria could feel a greater relief from the tenseness that had built up inside her. Their conversation moved on to other things.

That night, hiding behind the sofa, she'd feared that Minnie and her mother were dead, and had also feared for her own life. Luckily, though, Evan fell asleep not long after he sat down. His loud snoring rumbled, and sent vibrations through the fabric of the sofa. Slowly, Victoria began to believe it would be safe to make an escape.

Walking out from her hiding place, concentrating hard on getting away, she almost keeled over, unaware she had been holding her breath for fear of waking Evan. Struggling to draw in air, while at the same time trying not to make any noise, she shuffled out of the living room.

From the corner of her eye, Jane and Minnie could be seen sprawled out on the floor in the hallway. Not brave enough to look at them, she left the house and ran all the way home. *Maybe I should call an ambulance. No, I shouldn't get involved. They might be dead. No, they'll be fine.* Unpleasant thoughts bombarded her brain, but she batted them away like balls off a tennis racket, not wanting to think.

That night, Victoria cried herself to sleep. Too afraid to tell anyone what had happened, the events remained locked inside her head where they repeatedly replayed and hounded her. Guilt and self-reproach were constant companions.

There was nothing mentioned in the local paper or the local news on TV; she expected there would have been if Minnie and Jane were dead. *No news is good news*, she kept telling herself. Feeling sick to the stomach, she remembered Minnie's limp body, Jane trying to revive her, and the harrowing screams when Evan began hitting his wife.

In the days that followed, Victoria almost phoned the police a few times, but whenever she reached for the phone, her imagination would run wild; she'd begin to worry about having to step into a witness box and give evidence against Evan while he sat in court, his deep brown eyes boring deep into her soul warning her of the vengeance to come.

She'd searched the Internet for the contact details of Social Services, wanting to help Minnie, but couldn't bring herself to follow through. She'd only been fourteen years-old at the time, and not a very confident child.

Jane's phone call the next week brought great relief. Victoria didn't believe the excuse about Evan's rage being caused by mixing medication with alcohol, but made up her mind to believe it; that way she could move on in her own life and stop worrying about little Minnie. *It's none of my business*, she repeated over and over, as if trying to convince herself.

'So, where would you like to go tonight? There's a good film at the cinema I want to see...'

Adrian's words moved them further and further from the mystery of 25 Turner Avenue. Soon they'd be back in Hertfordshire, leaving this behind. Maybe it was for the best. The likelihood was that someone had been killed in that house. *Not Minnie, please not Minnie*, she heard her inner child's plea.

Just then, a young boy shouted out from across the road; he must have been about nine or ten years old. 'Ade! Hi, what's up?'

'Hi, Jamie,' said Adrian, twisting towards where the voice had come from. He waved at the boy.

'Visiting your parents?' asked Jamie.

'Yeah, just been.'

The young boy crossed the road and nodded politely at Victoria.

'Oh, this is Jamie, he lives across the road,' said Adrian to Victoria. 'This is Vicky, my girlfriend.' He smiled at Jamie.

'Nice to meet you, Vicky,' said Jamie, grinning.

'Hi,' she said, smiling back at him.

The young boy looked familiar. Curly brown hair; brown, nearly-black eyes. Evan. He looked like Evan. Victoria shivered.

'Do you want to come to ours for a cup of tea?' asked Jamie.

'No thanks, we've been stuffed full of food and tea by my mum,' said Adrian, laughing and rubbing his tummy.

Jamie joined in with the laughter.

Victoria faked a laugh too as she studied with intrigue the boy's features, sure he was one of the Baker children.

'Your mum's a good cook,' said Jamie. 'She made us dinner last week when Nan was ill. Sure you don't wanna come in for a bit?'

'Sorry, but we were hoping to catch a film at the cinema; it'll be starting soon.' Adrian checked his watch as he spoke.

'Okay.' The young boy hung his head, but when he looked back at them he was smiling. 'Maybe next time you're around? Nan would love to meet your girlfriend,' he said to Adrian. 'Oh, and I've got a new computer game I wanna show you. I'll beat you at this one. I'm an expert!'

'Ha, ha! You'll never beat me at computer games. It's about time you stopped trying!'

'I bet I will,' said Jamie, laughing.

'Okay, I'll come round next time I'm in town.'

'Cool!'

Victoria stood silently throughout the exchange, mainly staring at Jamie. A couple of times, he caught her eye and looked away, and she realised she'd been studying him too intently.

'Well, I'd better get back,' said the boy, finally, holding up a carrier bag. 'I need to get these to Nan; she's cooking dinner.'

'Okay, it was nice to see you again, Jamie boy, take care.'

'You should visit more,' said Jamie as he waved to both of them and dodged a car, crossing back to the other side of Turner Avenue.

'Nice boy,' said Adrian, when Jamie was out of earshot.

'Yeah, you seem to get on well,' commented Victoria, still curious about the boy.

'Yeah, he's so sweet. Hard to believe, considering who his dad was.'

Was? Was Evan dead? Did the excessive drink (and maybe drugs) get to him eventually? wondered Victoria.

'What do you mean?' she asked, not sure if she really wanted to hear the answer.

'His dad used to beat up his mum, and nearly killed Jamie and his sisters a few times,' replied Adrian. 'All I remember him as was an old drunk who used to shout a lot, sitting outside their house, even in the rain sometimes. Their windows used to get broken a lot, too. Their neighbour is a good friend of my mum, and she always complained that she heard arguing in that house all the time.

'I always found Jamie's dad a bit intimidating, and remember Mrs Baker—that's Jamie's mum—used to have cuts and bruises on her arms and face sometimes.'

Victoria's eyebrows rose as she listened with interest.

'I moved away years ago,' continued Adrian, 'but soon after I moved, I was visiting my parents one weekend, and found the whole road cordoned off. Apparently, Evan—Jamie's dad—went crazy with a knife and killed his wife.'

Victoria gasped.

'I know.' Adrian nodded. 'It's like something from a horror movie. Anyway, he went to prison and his wife's mum—a widow—moved in to look after the kids. They were nearly put into care after what happened.'

Victoria pictured little Minnie's face. A sadness engulfed her. *I should have done something...* The familiar tug of guilt returned.

'So, Mrs Baker's dead?' she said, in disbelief, thinking aloud.

'Yeah, those poor kids have been through a lot.'

'Well, at least he's in prison now, I suppose,' said Victoria, thinking of how terrified she had been that night all those years ago, crouched behind the sofa.

'No, last year he got out of jail and came back,' said Adrian.

'He's around?' Victoria looked behind her, as if worried he would be following them; an irrational feeling that she found hard to shake.

'No. Not anymore.' Adrian frowned as he continued, 'I only know this from third-hand information, so a lot of it might be gossip, but apparently he was sorry for what he did—he hadn't meant to kill his wife. He was clean... off the drink, since he went into prison. His mother-in-law felt sorry for him and let him stay with them. Two months later, he was found dead.'

Victoria's mouth fell open. 'What happened?'

'The postmortem found he was poisoned. His daughter confessed to her nan that she'd put rat poison in his food. Wanted him dead. Minnie's nan didn't want her to end up in a young offender's institution, so she told the police *she'd* poisoned Evan to protect the kids; said she did it in self-defence. If their nan had gone to jail, the kids would have been put into care. Somehow she got away with a suspended sentence—probably because of his history.'

'Oh my God, those poor children.' There were tears in Victoria's eyes. That little child grew up to be a murderer, and she could have prevented it... maybe... Two people were dead. The children were orphans. Minnie must have gone through hell all those years if she'd ended up feeling that the only way out was to kill him. *If only I'd said something.*

'They're all so sweet,' said Adrian. 'Minnie is a great girl. I'm glad she wasn't arrested. She's such a good influence on the younger kids. Like a mum to them.

'I once asked her what it's like living with him drunk all the time. She was only a kid. Minnie told me about a nice lady who used to babysit her when she was little. The babysitter once read her a story about a girl who was in danger but knew how to survive. She says that she always remembered that story. When things got bad she did what the little girl had done: played dead. Makes me shiver just thinking about what he put them through.'

"*The Giant and the Poison Berry*", thought Victoria, eyes wide.

‘She told me she always remembered the lady who read her that story, like she was an angel or her fairy godmother; said that story was the reason she survived all those years.’ He sighed.

The little girl slipped the juice from the poisonous berry into the giant’s drink, and he took a huge slurp and fell down onto the floor, dead...

Victoria shed a tear and took Adrian’s hand. He frowned and put an arm around her as they continued to walk away from the house.

Thank you for reading!

More books by Maria Savva:

Novels:

Coincidences,
A Time to Tell,
Second Chances,
The Dream,
Haunted

Novella:

Cutting the Fat (with co-author Jason McIntyre)

Short story collections:

Pieces of a Rainbow,
Love and Loyalty (and Other Tales),
Fusion,
Delusion and Dreams

For news, excerpts, book trailers, and more, please see the official website: http://www.mariasavva.com

www.ingramcontent.com/pod-product-compliance
Ingram Content Group UK Ltd.
Pitfield, Milton Keynes, MK11 3LW, UK
UKHW041901190726
13854UKWH00003B/1011